**The playful text — perfect for reading aloud — and whimsical watercolors are sure to entice even the most reluctant sleepyhead into bed.**

"The little girl is about to tuck herself in when she notices that "everyone" else is missing. Running from place to place in her cozy timbered house, she gathers half a dozen toys . . . The role reversal is a grand way to put the child vicariously in charge of the bedtime ritual. . . . Simple, repetitive, and reassuring; a perfect bedtime book."
—*Kirkus Reviews*

". . . a top-notch pre-bed book that depicts a young girl's progressive nighty-night. . . . Exquisite watercolors of the little girl's search for pals such as Zoe the doll or Oscar the clown, as well as scenes of tooth brushing and potty visiting, will be cozily familiar to any toddler."
—*Boston Herald*

Text and illustrations copyright © 1993
L'École des Loisirs, Paris, France.

English text and translation copyright © 1994
Chronicle Books.

First published in the United States in 1994 by Chronicle Books.

Originally published in French under the title *Bonne Nuit!* by
Pastel, an imprint of L'École des Loisirs, Paris.

Calligraphy and typography by Laura Jane Coats.

Library of Congress Cataloging-in-Publication Data:
Masurel, Claire.
[*Bonne nuit!*]
Good night! / by Claire Masurel; illustrated by Marie H. Henry.
p.        cm.
"Originally published in French under the title *Bonne nuit!*" — T. p. verso.
Summary: A little girl gathers her toys together in preparation for bedtime.
ISBN 0-8118-1169-7 (pbk.)
[1. Bedtime — Fiction.]  I. Henry, Marie H., ill.  II. Title.
PZ7.M4239584Go      1994
[E] — dc20      93-30198      CIP      AC

Distributed in Canada by Raincoast Books
8680 Cambie Street, Vancouver, B.C. V6P 6M9

10  9  8  7  6  5  4

Chronicle Books
85 Second Street, San Francisco, California 94105

www.chroniclebooks.com/Kids

Printed in Singapore

# Good Night!

written by
**CLAIRE MASUREL**

illustrated by
**MARIE H. HENRY**

chronicle books·san francisco

It's getting dark. Look at the sky.
The moon is shining. The stars are twinkling.
It's time to go to bed.

Fluff up the pillows. Pull down the covers.
But wait! Where is everyone?

Zoe!
Oscar!
Jojo!
Daisy!
Max!
Theo!

Where are you?

Silly Max.
It's not time to eat!
It's time to go to bed.

Silly Oscar.
It's not time to play cards!
It's time to go to bed.

Silly Zoe.
It's not time to read stories!
It's time to go to bed.

Silly Theo.
It's not time to watch television!
It's time to go to bed.

Silly Jojo.
It's not time to play hide-and-seek!
It's time to go to bed.

But wait!

There is still someone missing.

Where can she be? Maybe she's in the bathroom.

There you are, silly Daisy.

It's not bathtime.
It's time to go to bed!

At last,
everyone is tucked in.

**CLAIRE MASUREL** was born in Normandy, France and lived in New York City for fifteen years before moving to Italy. She is the author and illustrator of over fifteen books for children, and has also illustrated many other books. *Good Night!* is her first collaboration with Mary H. Henry.

**MARIE H. HENRY** lived in France, where she studied music at the National Conservatory at Versailles. When her children were born, she found that her music woke them, so she turned her attention to watercolors. She created her first book as a gift for her daughter.